Movie Adaptation by
Tracey West

SCHOLASTIC INC.
New York   Toronto   London   Auckland   Sydney
Mexico City   New Delhi   Hong Kong

ISBN 0-439-29487-8

12 11 10 9 8 7 6 5   1 2 3 4 5 6/0

Printed in the U.S.A.
First Scholastic printing, April 2001

*S*pell *of the Unown* takes place in the Johto region, a new land that Pokémon trainer Ash Ketchum and his friends are just starting to explore.

The Johto region is home to many new Pokémon. Here's a sneak peek at the new Pokémon who star in this book:

Chikorita: This Grass Pokémon is light-green, with a green leaf on top of its head. Its attacks include Razor Leaf and Vine Whip.

Cyndaquil: This Fire Pokémon may look cute, but it packs a powerful Flamethrower Attack.

Totodile: This Water Pokémon has sharp

teeth and a spike on the end of its sharp tail. Watch out for its Water Gun Attack!

Noctowl: This Flying Pokémon has gold-and-red feathers. It is the evolved form of Hoothoot.

Aipom: It's cute and agile. Aipom has a hand on the end of its tail that it can use to grab things.

Flaaffy: This little Pokémon is cuddly and pink, but its attacks may surprise you — Flaaffy is an Electric Pokémon.

Teddiursa: This little guy isn't like any teddy bear you've ever seen. For one thing, its punch can knock you off your feet!

Phanpy: Phanpy has a long trunk and sturdy body. It evolves into Donphan.

Kingdra: You've heard of Seadra and Seaking, right? Well, this is their evolved form.

Mantine: This Water Pokémon also has the ability to fly.

Entei: This Pokémon looks like a large, majestic beast with a shaggy mane. It is known only in legend.

The Unown: These mysterious Psychic Pokémon have strange powers. They come in 26 different shapes that resemble the letters of the alphabet.

Chapter One
Discovering the Unown

"Tell me a story, Daddy," said the little girl. She snuggled under her blanket and gazed at her father with pleading gray eyes.

Her father, Professor Hale, smiled. He sat on the edge of the bed. "Of course, Molly," he said. He opened up a storybook, Molly's favorite. "These are legendary Pokémon, Molly. Lots of people believe in them, even though they've never seen them. And in this book, the artist imagined what some of them might look like."

The first picture showed a dark sky. Hundreds of small Pokémon swirled in the air. A white light glowed behind their strange shapes. To Molly they looked something like the letters in the alphabet.

"That's the Pokémon you're looking for, right, Dad?" Molly asked.

Professor Hale nodded. "That's right. This Pokémon is called the Unown. It has mysterious powers."

Molly shivered. The Unown looked funny. She turned the page. "I like this one better," she said.

This picture showed a strong-looking Pokémon standing in front of a beautiful palace made of crystal. The Pokémon stood on four legs and was covered in shaggy reddish-brown fur. White fur covered its muzzle and cascaded down its back.

"Entei, one of the legendary Pokémon," said Hale. "Why do you like Entei so much?"

"Entei's big and strong but still nice," said Molly. "Just like you, Papa."

Professor Hale's dark eyes twinkled. "Wouldn't that be something if I were Entei?" He growled and got down on all fours.

Molly laughed. Her father's long hair made him look almost like Entei. She jumped on her father's back. Hale bounded around the room.

"Pidgey! Pidgey!"

Molly knew that sound. It was the alarm on her dad's laptop computer. It sounded just like the Flying Pokémon called Pidgey.

Hale placed Molly back on the bed and went to the computer. The face of a young man appeared. It was Schuyler, Professor Hale's assistant. He lived at Hale Mansion with Molly and her father.

"We have found something at the research site," Schuyler said. He sounded excited. "It may be a clue about the Unown."

"I'll be right there," Hale said.

Molly frowned. Her dad was always working.

Hale saw her expression. "I'm sorry, Molly," he said. "I'll be back as soon as I can. I'll miss you. Just keep me close in your dreams." Then he kissed his daughter good-bye and left.

Molly sighed and looked at her nightstand. Her dad might be at work, but she could always look at his picture. There he was, holding her when she was just a tiny baby. And there was her mom. She had been gone for so long now that Molly didn't even remember her.

There was another picture, too. This one showed baby Molly and her dad with a man in a white lab coat. Molly knew this was Professor Oak, her dad's old teacher. There was also a boy with black hair. Her dad said his name was Ash. And a pretty woman was hugging Ash. Molly guessed she was Ash's mother. She didn't really remember them, either.

While Molly dreamed, Professor Hale drove to the research site. Schuyler met him at the entrance to a cave. Hale and his team had been exploring the underground passages, hoping to find a portal to the world of the Unown. Hale felt they were getting closer each day.

"You're not going to believe this," Schuyler said. He led the professor down a dark passage and into a large room. Hale held up his lantern.

"The Unown!" Hale gasped. The walls were covered with pictures of the strange Pokémon. They looked almost like hieroglyphics carved into the walls.

"I've never seen markings like this before but they seem to be about the Unown,"

Schuyler said. "If anyone can figure out what this says, it's you."

Professor Hale took out a digital camera and began recording the images directly into his laptop computer. Schuyler studied the wall on the other side of the room.

Professor Hale's hands shook as he worked. This was his most exciting discovery yet. Then his lantern illuminated an object on the floor. Hale moved toward it.

It was a small wooden box. Hale opened the lid. Inside were wooden tiles. Each one was inscribed with a different Unown character.

"Amazing," Hale whispered. He picked up one of the tiles.

A high-pitched sound filled the air for a split second, and then an astonishing sight met Hale's eyes. The Unown on the tile became three-dimensional. The strange shape floated in the air in front of him. Hale reached out to grab it, but it disappeared in an instant.

Hale blinked. Had he imagined it? He reached into the box and grabbed a handful of tiles.

More Unown appeared. They swirled in a circle around him. Hale froze, stunned at the sight.

Then he vanished.

Schuyler heard a clatter as the wooden box crashed to the ground. He turned away from the wall. The room was empty except for the box and Hale's computer.

"Professor! Professor!" Schuyler cried, but he felt his stomach tighten as he realized the truth.

"The Unown," Schuyler whispered. "The Unown have taken him."

Then he turned and ran as fast as he could.

Chapter Two

Powers Unleashed

The next morning Molly walked into the dining room, clutching her storybook. She hoped her dad was home. Maybe they could finish reading the book together.

But Hale wasn't there. Schuyler sat at the table, talking to the butler. They both looked very sad.

"Where's Papa?" Molly asked.

Schuyler picked up Molly. "Something happened at the research site, Molly," he told her. "But don't worry. We'll take care of you."

Molly felt scared. Really scared.

"Where is Papa?" she asked again.

"We do not know, Miss," the butler said sadly. "He is gone."

Schuyler placed Molly down. He handed her the wooden box and the computer.

"These are all we found," he said.

Molly did not want to listen. "Papa is not gone! He is coming home!" She ran into her father's office and slammed the door.

Molly sat on the floor and turned on the computer.

"Come on, Papa," Molly said. "I know you sent me an e-mail."

But no e-mail appeared. Instead, Molly saw the photos her father had taken of the Unown markings the night before.

"Those are the Pokémon Papa was looking for," Molly said.

Molly's elbow accidentally nudged the box. The lid flew open, and the tiles spilled out.

"Unown," Molly said. "I can spell our names with the Unown."

Molly spread out the tiles on the floor in front of her. They really did look like letters. Molly used the tiles to spell out three words.

"Mama. Papa. Molly," she said quietly. She touched the letters with her fingertips.

At Molly's words, the ceiling opened up

above her. A whirling funnel of wind appeared over her head. The Unown swirled inside the funnel, like they were dancing.

They're real, Molly thought. *Papa was right!*

The Unown swirled down and circled Molly.

For a moment, Molly forgot about her sadness. The dance looked so beautiful.

Then something amazing happened. The floor around Molly turned into shimmering crystal. The crystal spread, like liquid, to each corner of the room. Then the crystal covered the walls and the ceiling.

Schuyler burst through the door. "Molly! What is happening?"

A sheet of crystal shot up in front of Schuyler, securely blocking the door.

That was fine with Molly. The crystal looked so pretty. She did not want anyone to stop it.

Then, with a pang of sadness, Molly remembered her missing father again. Even the Unown could not make her forget that. Molly opened up the storybook to the picture of Entei. The Pokémon reminded her so much of her father.

"Come back, Papa," Molly whispered. "Please come back to me."

At Molly's words, the Unown's dance got faster and faster. The Pokémon seemed to chatter in high-pitched voices.

A glowing light appeared next to Molly. She watched as the light took the shape of a Pokémon. Molly saw four strong legs. A shaggy back. A kind face crowned by white fur.

"Entei?" Molly said, with wonder in her voice.

"I am Entei. Are you the one who called me here?" Entei asked.

Molly nodded. "Papa, it's you!" she said. "You look just like the Entei in the story-book but it's really *you!*"

Entei bowed its shaggy head. "Your papa?" said Entei. "If that is what you wish. I will take care of you."

Molly ran and buried her head in Entei's soft fur.

Above her, the Unown continued their dance.

Around her, the crystal spread through every room in Hale Mansion, and out into the world. . . .

Chapter Three
Battle Time

Not far away, Pokémon trainer Ash Ketchum walked down a dirt road. His friends walked by his side. Orange-haired Misty was a Pokémon trainer, too. She specialized in Water Pokémon, and always carried Togepi, an eggshell Pokémon, with her. Togepi's tiny head, hands, and feet popped out of a colorful eggshell.

Ash's friend Brock used to be a gym leader. The boy had wavy brown hair and gave Ash good advice about raising Pokémon.

And then there was Pikachu. Ash's little yellow Pokémon never left his side. And

Pikachu's powerful Electric Attacks were always getting Ash out of trouble.

Step by step, Ash, Misty, and Brock continued their Pokémon journey. They wondered what adventure awaited them as they traveled toward the unknown, never suspecting that's exactly where this road would lead. A girl with long black hair walked toward them. She wore jeans, a red shirt, and a red-and-white hat that looked like a Poké Ball. That could only mean one thing.

"Hey, there. Are you a Pokémon trainer?" Ash asked.

The girl nodded. A Pokémon swung down from a nearby tree and landed on her shoulder. The purple Pokémon had a friendly face and big ears. Ash noticed something that looked like a hand on the end of its tail.

"I'm Lisa, and this is Aipom," said the girl. "What do you say? Wanna battle?"

Ash knew the invitation was a friendly one. Pokémon trainers often battled each other to practice so they could become better trainers. It was a good workout for their Pokémon, too.

"Okay. It will help me stay in shape for

my next Johto League match," Ash said with a smile.

Ash and Lisa walked down the road to a playground. They faced each other across the open space.

"Let's start this thing," Lisa said. "Go, Granbull!"

Lisa threw a Poké Ball, and a pink Poké-mon popped out. Granbull had a squat body and two strong legs. Two long teeth curved from its bottom jaw.

Granbull's fierce appearance didn't worry Ash. He threw out a Poké Ball of his own.

"Totodile, I choose you!" Ash cried.

A blue-green Pokémon exploded from the ball. The Water Pokémon had large jaws with rows of sharp teeth.

Granbull didn't wait. It lowered its head and charged at Totodile.

Totodile quickly dodged out of the way. Granbull growled and charged again. Totodile darted aside.

"Totodile, Water Gun!" Ash yelled.

Totodile shot a powerful stream of water out of its mouth. The water blast knocked Granbull flat on its back.

"Granbull, return!" Lisa cried. She held out Granbull's Poké Ball, and a beam of red light shot out. Granbull disappeared into the ball.

Ash waited to see what Lisa would do next.

"Go, Girafarig!" yelled Lisa.

A strange-looking Pokémon appeared. Girafarig walked on four graceful legs. It had a long, slender neck. The front half of its body was yellow with black spots. Its hind legs were black, and its tail had a weird, smiling face on the end.

Ash didn't know what to expect from Girafarig. He decided it was best to use a fresh Pokémon. He recalled Totodile and threw out another Poké Ball. "Chikorita, I choose you!"

Chikorita was pretty strange-looking itself. The light-green Grass Pokémon had four short, stubby legs and a smooth round head. Green spots ringed its neck, and a green leaf sprouted from the top of its head.

Girafarig made the first move. It leaped up high in the air. Chikorita dodged out of the way before Girafarig landed.

Chikorita fought back with Vine Whip. Vines shot out of two of the spots around its neck. The vines lashed at Girafarig. But Lisa's Pokémon jumped to the side, avoiding the vines.

Then Girafarig faced Chikorita. A rainbow-colored beam poured from its eyes.

That's a Psybeam, Ash realized. *A powerful Psychic Attack. Chikorita won't be able to take that!*

"Chikorita, jump!" Ash yelled.

Chikorita jumped out of the way. Then the leaf on top of its head began to spin. Sharp leaves spun out, slicing into Girafarig.

The Razor Leaf Attack shook Girafarig but didn't stop it. Girafarig countered with another Psybeam.

This time the rainbow beam hit its mark. Chikorita started to reel back and forth. Then it fell to the ground in a faint. Ash called it back safely inside its Poké Ball.

Lisa smiled triumphantly and recalled Girafarig. She didn't throw a Poké Ball this time. Instead, Aipom jumped off her shoulder.

"Noctowl, I choose you!" Ash cried, throwing another Poké Ball.

A Flying Pokémon flew out and up into the sky. Noctowl had gold-and-red feathers, a powerful beak, and red markings around its eyes.

Aipom climbed up onto the monkey bars in the playground and taunted Noctowl.

Noctowl swooped down from the sky and lunged at Aipom with its claws. Aipom grabbed the bars with its tail and swung out of the way.

That didn't stop Noctowl. The Flying Pokémon swooped down again. This time, it grabbed Aipom before it could react. Noctowl flew high into the sky. Then it dropped Aipom into Lisa's arms. The little Pokémon looked too rattled to battle anymore.

"Good work, Noctowl!" Ash returned the Flying Pokémon to its Poké Ball and sent out Bulbasaur. The Grass Pokémon had a short, sturdy body and a large head. A plant bulb grew from its back.

Meanwhile, Butterfree appeared at Lisa's side. The Bug Pokémon had large white wings and big red eyes.

Bulbasaur made the first move. The plant bulb on its back opened up, and two green vines lashed out. Butterfree quickly flew out of their path.

"Butterfree, use Sleep Powder," Lisa called out.

Then Butterfree flapped its wings, and a shimmering powder filled the air. Bulbasaur's eyes started to droop.

Ash knew Bulbasaur couldn't respond until the powder wore off. He started to call back Bulbasaur, but Butterfree wasn't finished. The Bug Pokémon furiously flapped its wings, creating a whirlwind. Bulbasaur tumbled across the road and landed at Ash's feet.

Lisa jumped up and down triumphantly. Then she recalled Butterfree and sent out Mankey in its place. The Fighting Pokémon had a round, fuzzy body, a piglike snout, and powerful arms and legs.

Ash sent out Cyndaquil to face Mankey. The Fire Pokémon had a long snout. The top of its squat body was blue, and its underbelly was white. Red flames shot out of Cyndaquil's back when it attacked.

Cyndaquil and Mankey charged at each other. They slammed together, and each one fell backward.

Cyndaquil got to its feet first. Red-hot flames sizzled on its back. The Fire Pokémon opened its mouth wide and blasted Mankey with a Flamethrower Attack.

That was all it took. Mankey was out.

"We're just about even so far," Ash called to Lisa. "Let's finish this. One more round."

Lisa nodded and threw one last Poké Ball. Quagsire popped out. The chubby Water Pokémon was shaped like a pear. It had smooth blue skin, a flat tail, and walked upright on two flat feet.

"Pikachu, I choose you!" Ash yelled.

Pikachu ran in front of Ash. It focused all its energy on building up a powerful Electric Attack.

"Pikachuuuuuu!" A bolt of electric lightning exploded from Pikachu and rocked Quagsire.

Quagsire's a Water Pokémon, Ash thought smugly. *This Electric Attack should end this now.*

But Quagsire didn't flinch. The Electric

Attack fizzled out. Quagsire stood there, calmly smiling.

"That must be a pretty high level Quagsire," Brock remarked. "Any other Water Pokémon would have succumbed to that attack."

Ash tried another approach. "Pikachu, Tackle!"

Pikachu ran at Quagsire as fast as it could. The Water Pokémon held out a hand. Pikachu collided with it and bounced right back to Ash.

Quagsire opened its mouth and sent a stream of water at Pikachu. Pikachu jumped up onto a swing set to avoid the blast. Then it took a powerful leap and landed headfirst right on top of Quagsire's head. The Water Pokémon collapsed in a heap.

"Awesome Head Butt, Pikachu!" Ash said proudly, "We won!"

But the attack was hard on Pikachu. The little yellow Pokémon slid to the ground.

Lisa smiled and held out her hand. "Great battle," she said. "I have to admit, I'm impressed, Ash."

"Thanks, Lisa, but you almost beat me," Ash said.

"This is Ash's fifth battle this week," Misty said. "His Pokémon are getting pretty tired."

"Lisa, you you happen to know if there's a Pokémon Center anywhere around here?" asked Brock.

"There's one just over the mountain," Lisa said, "in Greenfield."

Misty brightened. "Greenfield? That's supposed to be a beautiful little town with beautiful gardens and a beautiful mountain with a beautiful mansion right at the top."

Ash shrugged. "As long as there's a Pokémon Center there, I don't care what it looks like."

"Then follow me," Lisa said. "I know the quickest way to get there."

Lisa and Aipom led them down the road. The walk passed quickly as Lisa and Ash compared battle stories.

Soon they came to the top of a hill. Ash could make out roads and buildings in the valley below.

"You can see Greenfield from the top of the hill," Lisa said. Then she gasped.

"What is it?" Ash asked.

Then he saw it. A huge structure sat in the middle of the town. Two blue crystal towers glittered in the sky. The towers were surrounded by hundreds of giant pieces of pink crystal. The pink pieces looked like flower petals.

"That used to be Hale Mansion," Lisa said, "but Hale Mansion never looked like that."

Then Ash noticed something else. The crystal seemed to be moving. In front of their eyes, the crystal slowly spread across the fields of grass and flowers. Everything it touched turned to icy, smooth glass.

"What's going on here?" Ash wondered.

Chapter Four

Kidnapped

"Let's get to the Pokémon Center," Lisa said. "It's at the edge of the village. Maybe we can find out what happened."

Ash and the others agreed. As they hurried away, the crystal mansion loomed in the distance. Ash had a hard time keeping his eyes off the place. There was something mysterious about it.

Finally they reached the Pokémon Center. Police cars and news vans surrounded the building, and a crowd of people milled about. Ash saw Officer Jenny, a blue-haired police officer, trying to organize everyone.

"Ash? Is that you?" a woman asked.

Ash stopped in his tracks. It couldn't be!

22

He turned around. A pretty brown-haired woman stood next to a gray-haired man wearing a white lab coat.

"Mom! Professor Oak! What are you doing here?" Ash asked. He hugged his mom.

Ash's mom, Delia, nodded toward Hale Mansion. "I've known Professor Hale for years. He used to study Pokémon at Professor Oak's lab."

"Then he moved away and became a famous Pokémon expert, right Mom?" Ash said. He remembered that Professor Hale brought his daughter to visit them a few years ago.

"Spencer Hale was one of Professor Oak's best students. His wife disappeared two years ago while searching for a mysterious Pokémon artifact on an archaeological expedition. Hale has been trying to solve the mystery of her disappearance ever since."

Delia put an arm around her son. "First Spencer's wife disappeared and now all this happens."

"It's weird," Brock said. Ash, Pikachu, Misty, Brock, and Lisa settled outside at a picnic table with Delia and Professor Oak.

"*Pika, pikachu.*" Ash turned at the

sound of his Pokémon's voice. Pikachu was staring out into the field next to them. Its pointy ears twitched.

Ash looked up. Some kind of Pokémon was running toward them. But it didn't look like any Pokémon normally found in a field, like a Rattata or a Pidgey. This was much bigger.

As the Pokémon got closer, Ash saw that it looked like a shaggy beast. He had never seen anything like it before. Every time the Pokémon's feet touched the ground, a sharp crystal shard sprung up underneath it.

"It can't be . . . it looks like Entei," Professor Oak whispered behind him.

Entei landed on the ground in front of Delia. Ash hesitated. Was this Pokémon friendly? It didn't look like it was going to attack them.

Entei stared into Delia's eyes. Then it spoke in a deep voice. "I have come for you. Molly needs a Mama."

Delia's eyes grew round. "Take me . . . to . . . her . . ." she said in a sleepy voice.

It's almost like she's hypnotized, Ash thought. He jumped out of his seat.

"Hey, what are you — "

Ash was too late. His mom fainted, falling across Entei's back. Without another word, Entei turned around and bounded away from the Pokémon Center.

"Pika!" Pikachu sprang into action. It leaped up and grabbed Entei's furry tail.

Ash and Brock ran after Entei. Pikachu was still hanging on. Ash saw sparks dance on Pikachu's cheeks.

"Pikachuuuu!" The Electric Pokémon attacked Entei with a Thundershock. But the attack didn't seem to affect Entei at all. Entei stopped for a second and shrugged off Pikachu. Then it leaped away.

Ash caught up to Pikachu and picked it up. "Pikachu, are you okay?"

Pikachu nodded. *"Pika."*

Entei was bounding off again, getting farther away with each second. Ash started to run after it. But Brock held him back.

"Don't go, Ash," Brock said. "You don't know what's out there. Besides, there's no way to travel across that crystal."

Ash knew Brock was right. There was nothing he could do — not now, anyway.

"Don't worry, Mom!" Ash called after her. "I'll come get you. I'll figure out a way!"

Chapter Five
A Mom for Molly

Inside Hale Mansion, Molly sat at the foot of her bed. She stared at the screen of her father's computer. There she saw Entei returning to her with Ash's mother on its back.

"She looks like such a nice mama," Molly murmured.

Soon Entei stepped into the room. He knelt down, and Delia rolled off his back onto Molly's bed.

"I have brought you what you wished for," Entei said.

Delia's eyes fluttered, and she slowly sat up.

"You can be my mama now," Molly told her. "You can take care of me."

Delia looked at Molly and then at Entei, still dazed. The power of the Unown was clouding her mind.

"I . . . will . . . be . . . your . . . mama," Delia said slowly. She sounded as though she was hypnotized.

Molly hugged her tightly. "Oh, Mama. Entei, can we all stay together here forever?" asked the little girl.

"If that is what you wish," Entei said. "I only want you to be happy."

Entei padded over to the window on its soft paws. "Your world is growing wider. The crystal is spreading outside the mansion," Entei told Molly.

"It's so pretty," Molly said.

Not far away, three figures watched Hale Mansion through binoculars. The first was a girl with long red hair. The second was a purple-haired boy. The third was a Scratch Cat Pokémon with tan fur, triangle-shaped ears, and a long tail.

It was Team Rocket, a trio of trouble-makers. They were looking for valuable Pokémon to steal.

"Greenfield is just as I imagined it," said Jessie, the girl, "beautiful fields of flowers that turn into a bizarre crystal waste-land . . . Hey, what's going on?"

"There must be some valuable Pokémon inside," guessed James, the boy.

"Not only that, it looks ba-a-ad!" said Meowth, the Pokémon.

"Wobbuffet!" A tall blue Pokémon popped up next to Jessie and nodded its head. Wobbuffet had a bullet-shaped body, long arms, and a strange tail that dragged on the ground.

"Who told you to come out?" Jessie asked crossly. "I'm beginning to regret the day I ever caught you!"

"Wobb," replied Wobbuffet sadly.

"Stop whining, Jess," James said. "Let's figure out how to get inside!"

The mystery is about to begin . . .

Molly and her dad look at pictures of the legendary Pokémon Entei and the Unown. Lots of people believe in these Pokémon, even though they've never seen them.

But the Unown have come to life and they have entered the mansion where Molly lives.

Entei has entered our world as well. Molly loves the legendary Pokémon.

Then, the Unown Pokémon take over. They cover Molly's home with hard crystal.

Lisa

This is Lisa.

Aipom teases
Ash's Pokémon.

Granbull pounces on Ash's Totodile.

Girafarig
has powerful
Psychic Attacks.

battles Ash

Ash's Noctowl swoops down on Aipom.

Quagsire, the Water Fish Pokémon.

Pikachu and Ash are a winning team.

The Pokémon relax after a tough battle.

Lunch time! Togepi munches happily, but Pikachu senses danger.

Molly wants a mom. Entei kidnaps Ash's mom for Molly.

Ash has to save his mom.
He uses Water Pokémon
to break into the
crystal-covered mansion.

Ash's mom is
under a spell.
Now she thinks
she's Molly's
mom.

Molly

Flaafy may look cute, but it's got powerful Electric Attacks.

Teddiursa knocks out Vulpix with a Dynamic Punch.

vs. Brock

Phanpy ends the battle for Molly.

Team Rocket is on the hunt for valuable Pokémon. They'll blast their way into that mansion if they have to.

Molly takes

Kingdra slams into
Misty's Goldeen.

on Misty

"Mantine, use your Whirlpool!"

Misty's Staryu is ready for an underwater battle.

A little water can't keep Team Rocket out.

Ash has to face Entei to save his mom.

Ash vs.

Pikachu is no match for Entei's powerful attacks.

Charizard busts in to battle Entei and save the day.

Entei

Molly is ready to end the fighting, but the Unown can't stop.

The Unown trap Entei in a crystal cage.

Even Team Rocket wants to help.

The world is saved thanks to Ash and his friends.

Ash has done some brave things in the Johto region, but this adventure beats them all!

Chapter Six
Molly's Message

"Ash, the Pokémon that took your mother was Entei," said Professor Oak.

Ash, Pikachu, Misty, and Brock were gathered around Professor Oak inside the Pokémon Center. Professor Hale's assistant, Schuyler, was there, too.

"Entei is a legendary Pokémon," Oak went on. "No one has ever seen one before — until now."

"So how did Entei get there?" Ash wondered. "And why does it want my mom?"

"We're not sure," said Schuyler. "But the Unown are inside than mansion. They must have something to do with Entei's appearance. I know it's hard to believe, but there's no other explanation. First Professor Hale disappears, then this crystallization, and now Entei."

"The Unown *must* be behind it," said Professor Oak.

Ash felt panic rise inside him. "But Mom's in there. We have to help her!"

"Don't worry, Ash," Misty said soothingly. "They'll figure it out soon."

"*Pika pika,*" agreed Pikachu.

"Besides," Brock added. "The local police are working on finding a way in." He clicked on the television set.

Ash saw that a bulldozer was trying to break through the crystal. As the machine ploughed through the crystal field, a sound like breaking glass filled the air.

"It's working," Ash said hopefully.

But then, magically, sharp points of crystal rose from the ground among the shattered pieces. The crystal points easily knocked over the bulldozer. Ash saw the driver run out of the collapsed machine. Behind him, the bulldozer burst into flames.

Misty put an arm on Ash's shoulder. "They'll keep trying, Ash," she said.

"Ash, quick!" Professor Oak said. "I'm getting an e-mail from Hale Mansion."

Ash turned away from the television and leaned closer to the computer screen. A picture of a little girl with brown pigtails and gray eyes popped up.

"It's Molly!" Schuyler said.

"Why are you trying to get in?" Molly asked. "I am happy here. Mama and Papa and me just wanna stay by ourselves forever, so stay away! Leave us alone!"

The screen went blank.

"Did she just say her mother and her father were with her?" Professor Oak said.

"But what did she mean?" Misty asked. "You said Professor Hale disappeared, didn't you? And what about her mom?"

Ash knew just what Molly meant. Molly had his mother in there. And she wasn't going to give her back.

Ash knew what he had to do. And he wasn't going to let anyone talk him out of it. He quietly turned and headed for the door.

"Pika!" Pikachu ran up to him.

"I'm not gonna wait around anymore," Ash said. "Pikachu, it's up to us to save Mom on our own!"

Chapter Seven

The Secret of the Unown

Ash and Pikachu walked across the grass toward the crystal field.

"Ash, wait!"

Ash stopped at the sound of Misty's voice. She and Brock ran up to them.

"We're coming with you," Brock said. "We can't let you do this alone."

Ash nodded. He didn't want to put his friends in danger, but he knew there was no way of talking them out of it.

"Thanks, guys," Ash said.

Ash started to turn around again, but Aipom appeared on the road. It approached Ash and opened up the hand on the end of its tail. Inside was a small circle made of silver metal. In the center was a blank face, like a clock face. Ash had never seen it before.

Lisa was walking toward them. "If you're going to do something crazy," she said, "at least take my Poké Gear."

Ash took the Poké Gear from Aipom's tail. "What is it?" he asked.

"We use them all the time in the Johto region," she said. "You can use it to stay in touch with the Pokémon Center."

Ash looked at the device in his hand. "Cool! Thanks, Lisa." He slipped the Poké Gear into his vest pocket.

"Use it if you need help," Lisa said. Then she headed back to the Pokémon Center.

Ash took a deep breath. "Okay then. Let's go get my mom!"

The friends walked in silence over the grass. Then they reached the point where the crystal had taken over. Ash gingerly stepped onto the shiny surface.

It was like stepping on ice, way too slippery to walk across. And once they got across the field, they'd have to climb uphill to get to the mansion. That would be impossible.

And there was something else. The crystal almost seemed like it was alive — like it sensed they were there. A sharp crystal spear sprang up near where Ash's foot had touched down.

"It's impossible!" Ash said. "I wish I still had Charizard. I could climb on its back and just fly there."

Ash's Charizard was a huge Fire Pokémon that looked like a winged dragon. Ash had left in the Charicific Valley so it could train with other Charizard. Right now he was wishing he had kept Charizard with him.

"Maybe there's a way in," Brock said. "Let's walk around the edge of the crystal. Maybe we'll find something."

"Right," Ash said. He wasn't going to give up so easily.

They walked in silence around the crystal. Hale Mansion glittered on the hilltop above them.

"*Pikachu,*" Pikachu's ears twitched. It ran on ahead.

Ash and the others followed. Pikachu stopped at a swiftly running stream. The stream led across the field, all the way to the mansion.

"Amazing," Brock said. "The crystal doesn't seem to be affecting the water at all."

Ash jumped in. The water came up to his ankles. "Let's go!" Ash said.

The water was cold, but Ash didn't care. Each step took him closer to his mom.

As they walked, Ash got a closer look at what lay ahead. The stream wouldn't take him directly to the mansion. It led to a waterfall that ran down the hillside.

Ash stood at the bottom of the waterfall and looked up. At the top was a pond. Beyond that was Hale Mansion.

"We just need to get up there," Ash said. "But how?"

Brock looked thoughtful. "You might not have Charizard," he said. "But I bet your other Pokémon can help."

"Of course!" Ash said. He threw out three Poké Balls. There was a flash of light, and Noctowl, Bulbasaur, and Chikorita appeared.

"Noctowl, please carry Bulbasaur and Chikorita to the top of the waterfall," Ash told his Pokémon.

One at a time, Noctowl quickly carried the two Grass Pokémon to the top.

Ash called up to Bulbasaur and Chikorita. "Use your Vine Whips!"

Bulbasaur sent two strong green vines down the waterfall. Chikorita did the same.

"After you," Ash told Brock and Misty.

Ash's friends climbed up the vines. Then Pikachu jumped on Ash's back, and they climbed up the waterfall. Soon they had all reached the top.

"Thanks, guys," Ash said. He called Noctowl, Bulbasaur, and Chikorita back into their Poké Balls.

"What now?" Misty asked.

Ash scanned the landscape. They were standing at the edge of a pond. The pond led right to a greenhouse, which was attached to the mansion.

"I think we can get across the pond," Ash said. "Then we can find a way inside the greenhouse."

Before they could start, Ash heard a beeping noise from his pocket.

"The Poké Gear," Ash remembered. He took out the device. Professor Oak's face stared at him from the screen.

"Your climb up the waterfall made it on the television news," Oak said. "Congratulations, Ash."

Ash grimaced. He didn't want the professor to know what he was up to. "I'm sorry, Professor. I couldn't wait."

"I understand," Professor Oak said. "I have something important to tell you. Schuyler and I have been examining some of Professor Hale's research. We think we may have come up with an explanation for why all of this has been happening."

"What is it?" Ash asked.

"The Unown can read human minds," Professor Oak explained. "They can use human thoughts and dreams to change the world. The Unown may be tapping into the imagination of Professor Hale's daughter. The crystal fortress could be one of Molly's wishes made real."

"And Molly said she was lonely, so they sent her Entei. And a new mom," Misty chimed in.

"Exactly," said Professor Oak. "Do you realize what this means, Ash?"

"I think so," said Ash. "Whatever Molly wishes will become real."

"That is correct," said Professor Oak. "Which means that if Molly does not want you to take your mother back, the Unown will not allow you to. Be careful, Ash."

"I will," Ash said. He returned the Poké Gear to his pocket. Then he turned to Pikachu, Brock, and Misty.

"Let's find a way into this place," Ash said. "I can take whatever the Unown throw at me!"

Chapter Eight

Inside the Crystal Palace

Ash and the others sloshed through the pond. The water came up to their knees. They soon reached the greenhouse. The glass-walled building was now covered completely in crystal that shimmered in rainbow colors. The crystal blocked the door.

"Now what?" Misty asked.

Ash couldn't stand being so close without being able to get in. It was time for drastic measures.

"Let's blast our way in!" Ash cried. He threw out a Poké Ball. "Cyndaquil, Flamethrower!"

The Fire Pokémon burst out and landed on a crystal lily pad. Flames sprang from its back. Cyndaquil opened its mouth wide and shot a stream of flame through the crystal-covered door. The scorching flames burned a large round hole straight through it.

"All right!" Ash cheered. He started to step through the hole.

But the fire's power was fleeting. The crystal quickly began to grow again, covering the hole once more.

"Oh, no!" Ash cried. "We'll never get in."

Brock stared at the crystal barrier. Then he stared down at the pond below.

"Hmm. The crystal didn't affect the stream or the pond," Brock mused.

"Hey, that's right!" Misty said. "Maybe water is the key."

A plan flashed in Ash's mind. "I think I know what to do. We just need a little more firepower and some extra waterpower."

"No problem," said Misty and Brock together.

Brock took out a Poké Ball, and a small Pokémon appeared. It was brown with an orange, furry tail.

"Vulpix, help Cyndaquil. Blast the biggest hole you can," Brock said.

The Fire Pokémon nodded. Vulpix and Cyndaquil stood side by side and unleashed a fire blast at the same time. The flames burned a hole through the crystal, this time bigger than before.

Ash looked at Misty and nodded. They each threw out a Poké Ball. Ash's Totodile came out of one Poké Ball, and Misty's Staryu came out of the other. Staryu was shaped like a star with five pointed arms and a red gem in its middle.

"All right!" Ash yelled. "Totodile and Staryu will take over with Water Gun. The water will keep the hole open. We can swim through the water and get into the greenhouse that way."

Totodile aimed a powerful stream of water through the hole. Staryu did the same. Cyndaquil and Vulpix stopped their attack. The two Fire Pokémon jumped into the water stream and entered through the hole.

Pikachu dove through the water stream next. Brock followed, and then came Misty and Togepi. That left Ash, Totodile, and Staryu.

Ash thought about what to do. He couldn't go through and leave the Water Pokémon behind.

Then Ash had an idea. He grabbed Totodile underneath one of his arms and held Staryu underneath the other.

"Okay, guys," Ash said. "We're going in together."

Ash leaped forward and dove through the hole. Totodile and Staryu shot water the entire way. It worked! Ash, Totodile, and Staryu ended up on the greenhouse floor. Behind them, the crystal covered the hole once more.

Ash got to his feet. His whole body dripped with cold water. Ash didn't even feel it. He smiled at his friends.

"We're in!" Ash said triumphantly. "Let's go save my mom."

Ash may have made it inside Hale Mansion, but Team Rocket wasn't having the same kind of luck. The three thieves floated toward the mansion in a hot air balloon. The white balloon looked like a giant Meowth head.

"So how exactly are we supposed to get into the tower?" James asked.

Meowth held up its paws. Sharp claws sprang out. "Hey, it's the twerps. They're walking through a stream coming from that wacky building!" Meowth paused. "What's that?"

They turned toward the tower.

Entei stood on top of the glittering blue crystal. Its long white mane rippled in the wind.

"It looks scary. Do you think it will attack us?" James asked.

"It's probably harmless," Jessie said.

Jessie reached for a Poké Ball. She didn't even have time to throw it. Entei sent a huge ball of purple flame hurtling at the balloon.

"Look out!" Meowth cried. Team Rocket ducked. The fireball slammed into the balloon. It exploded into a thousand pieces.

The balloon spiraled downward. "Looks like Team Rocket's blasting off again!" they cried.

There was a splintering sound, and the balloon basket crashed through the roof of Hale Mansion. Jessie, James, and Meowth huddled together as the balloon landed with a thud.

The three villains slowly poked their heads out of the balloon basket. They were met with an astonishing sight.

Darkness surrounded them. Strange tendrils of crystal snaked up from the floor. The tendrils looked almost like gigantic green vines or branches.

"Well, we made it," Jessie said. "We're in the mansion."

"That's right," Meowth added. "But I don't like the looks of this place."

Chapter Nine

Molly's Latest Wish

Molly sat in her bedroom with the computer propped on her lap. Ash's mom sat by Molly's side, a distant look in her eyes. Entei watched over them both.

Now the computer showed Molly what was happening inside Hale Mansion. She watched as Ash and Staryu burst into the greenhouse.

"That boy is a Pokémon trainer," Molly said thoughtfully. "I think he and his Pokémon must be here in the house somewhere."

Entei stepped forward. "Shall I send them away?"

"I'd wanna be in a Pokémon battle,

45

Mama!" said the little girl. "But I don't know if I can do it."

"You can, if that is your wish," Entei said.

"Really?" asked Molly. "That would be so great, Mama. I could just imagine it — a Pokémon trainer. Papa, maybe I'm not old enough to have Pokémon yet!"

Entei nodded. "Do you *believe* you are old enough Molly," Entei asked.

"Yes, Papa!" Molly answered.

She rested her head on Delia's lap. "I want to be a great Pokémon trainer. I want to battle those kids," she said sleepily. Her eyes fluttered, and soon the girl was asleep.

Entei's solid body became transparent, and the Pokémon sank down through the floor. "It is done."

Chapter Ten

The Dream Battle Begins

Ash, Misty, and Brock called their Poké-mon back into their Poké Balls. Then Ash stepped through the back door of the greenhouse and into the mansion.

Ash wasn't prepared for what he saw next. He expected to see a big house filled with rooms and furniture. But the room they entered was covered with gleaming crystal, tinted milky white. A staircase rose straight up in front of them, but Ash couldn't see where it led to.

"We might as well try it," Misty said. "There's nowhere else to go."

Ash knew Misty was right. He only hoped that the staircase led to his mom.

Ash quickly led the way up the steps. Pikachu ran at his heels. Soon the floor seemed to be miles below him.

Suddenly, Ash felt a sinking feeling in his stomach. He looked down. The foundation of the staircase was disappearing with each step. Now the steps floated in the air, without any support at all. Each step seemed to float in the air. Ash stopped and tried not to look down.

"What's going on?" he called.

"Maybe the Unown are creating a new reality, just like Professor Oak said," Misty called back. "They're trying to stop you from reaching your mother."

"Whatever it is, we can't stop now!" Ash said. He ran up the floating stairs.

Finally, Ash reached the top. The stairs led up to a hole in the ceiling. A soft pink light shone through the hole. Ash stepped through.

Ash found himself in a beautiful green field filled with flowers of all colors. Another crystal staircase led up into a pink sky. Ash walked onto the field. Pikachu, Brock, and Misty followed.

"What now?" Ash wondered.

"Professor Oak said the Unown could make Molly's thoughts and dreams come to life," said Brock. "This must be part of Molly's dream world that the Unown created!"

"If this is Molly's dream, then where's Molly?" asked Ash.

At Ash's words, the sky opened up. Entei flew down through the sky. A young girl with brown pigtails sat on his back. But as Entei got closer to the ground, the girl transformed. Now she looked the same age as Brock. Her brown hair bounced on her shoulders, and she wore a blue dress.

The girl stepped off Entei's back and walked up to Ash.

"Let's have a Pokémon battle," she challenged him.

"I don't have time for a battle," Ash replied impatiently. He turned and faced Entei. "Where is my mother?"

Entei didn't answer.

Then Brock turned to Molly.

"You're Molly, aren't you?" he asked her.

Ash was puzzled. "I thought Molly was a little kid."

"Don't forget, Professor Oak said this is

Molly's dreamworld," Brock said. "The Un-own can make anything she wants come true."

Molly didn't seem interested in what Brock was saying. "Ash, are you going to battle me or not?" she asked.

Ash sighed. He wasn't sure what Molly was up to. But he didn't seem to have a choice.

"I'll do it," Ash said.

Brock stepped between them. "Don't waste your time battling *him* when you can battle *me*," Brock said.

Molly shrugged. "That's fine. I just want to battle."

Brock pulled Ash and Misty aside. "They both came down from that tower. That's gotta be where they've been keeping your mother," he whispered. "Go find her while I distract Molly."

Ash nodded. Brock was a good friend.

Ash, Misty, and Pikachu ran to the crystal staircase. Behind them, Brock faced Molly in her older dream form.

"All right," Brock said. "If you want a battle, I'll give you a battle!"

Chapter Eleven

Brock vs. Molly

"How about a standard battle?" Brock suggested. "Three Pokémon each."

"That's fine," said Molly, and as she spoke, the green grass underneath their feet disappeared and was replaced with sandy dirt. Now Brock faced Molly on a typical Pokémon battlefield. White lines formed a long rectangle on the field. In the center of the rectangle was a circle that looked like a Poké Ball. Each trainer's Pokémon would begin the battle inside this circle.

Brock threw a Poké Ball onto the field. The ball burst open, and a blue Pokémon with purple wings flew out.

"Go, Zubat!" yelled Brock.

Molly stood at the other end of the field with Entei at her side. She held out her hand, and a blue-and-white Poké Ball appeared there. She tossed the ball into the air.

"This is for luck. I choose Flaaffy!" called Molly.

Soft pink wool covered Flaaffy's cute little body. There were tufts of white fluffy wool on its head and around its neck. It had a striped, pointed tail with a blue ball on the end.

Brock made the first move. "Zubat, Super Sonic!"

Zubat flapped its wings, steadying itself in the air. It opened its mouth and waves of sonic energy escaped. Brock knew Super Sonic was always effective. The sonic waves couldn't be heard by the human ear, but the powerful vibrations usually weakened any Pokémon that came in contact with them.

Flaaffy was no different. The sonic waves bombarded the little Pokémon, and it reeled from the attack.

"It's working!" Brock yelled. "Zubat, Wing Attack."

Zubat flew in circles to gain speed. Then it swooped down, aimed right for Flaaffy.

"Evade it, Flaaffy!" Molly called out.

Flaaffy dodged out of Zubat's way just in time.

"Quick, Flaaffy. Thundershock!"

Thundershock? Flaaffy didn't look like any Electric Pokémon Brock had ever seen. He wasn't expecting that.

But it was true. Flaaffy blasted Zubat with a powerful jolt of electricity. Zubat was too surprised to get out of the way. It fluttered to the ground in a faint.

"Return, Zubat," Brock said, holding out Zubat's Poké Ball. "Good job."

Zubat disappeared, and Brock threw out another Poké Ball.

"This battle is just beginning. Go, Vulpix!" Brock yelled.

"Then I'll use this one," said Molly.

A Pokémon that looked like a cute brown teddy bear appeared. A swirl of white fur highlighted its round face.

"A Teddiursa, huh?" Brock mused. "It's almost as cute as you."

"It's more than just cute. Teddiursa, Dynamic Punch!" Molly cried.

Teddiursa ran up to Vulpix and delivered a powerful punch with its paw. The blow sent Vulpix tumbling backward.

"Vulpix, Quick Attack!" Brock yelled.

Vulpix scrambled back to its feet. It ran at Teddiursa with lightning speed.

Teddiursa easily jumped out of the way.

Molly shouted another command. "Teddiursa, Fury Swipes!"

Teddiursa assaulted Vulpix with one quick punch after another. Vulpix managed to run away, but not before a few of the punches made contact.

Vulpix faced Teddiursa across the field. Molly's Pokémon looked slightly weaker after delivering two attacks in a row.

"Vulpix!" The Fire Pokémon ran at Teddiursa. Brock could tell Vulpix was angry. Teddiursa ran toward Vulpix at the same time.

Slam! The two Pokémon collided in the middle of the field.

Teddiursa reeled from the collision but managed to stay on its feet. Vulpix wasn't so lucky. The Pokémon collapsed in a heap.

At this rate, the match may not last much

longer. Brock thought. *Molly's dreamed up Pokémon are tougher than the real ones!*

Brock knew he had to bring out his strongest Pokémon if he stood a chance of beating Molly. "Go, Onix!" Brock shouted, throwing a third Poké Ball.

A huge Pokémon appeared on the field. Onix, a rock snake Pokémon, had a body made out of boulders. Taking down Onix would be difficult, even for Molly.

But Molly didn't seemed concerned at all. "I choose Phanpy," she said, throwing out another blue-and-white Poké Ball.

The light blue Pokémon stood on four legs. It had round, floppy ears and a trunk. And it was small — about two feet high. Brock could not imagine what it could do against Onix.

"Phanpy, Rollout Attack!" Molly yelled.

Phanpy curled its body into a ball. It zipped across the field superfast. Onix didn't have time to react. Phanpy slammed into the Rock Pokémon, sending Onix flying across the field. Onix crashed into the ground and didn't move again.

Molly smiled. "You shouldn't let your

guard down just because your opponent is smaller," she said.

Brock was stunned. He wasn't sure what to say. He hadn't expected to lose to a little girl. He needed to give Ash more time to find his mom.

"Molly, how about another battle —" Brock began, but he was talking to no one. Molly and Entei had vanished.

While Brock and Molly were battling, Ash, Misty, and Pikachu climbed the crystal staircase. They didn't find Ash's mother, but they did find another dreamworld. This one had a sandy beach that led into a deep blue ocean. A warm breeze blew, and the sun shone overhead.

"What now?" Ash wondered aloud.

At the same moment, Molly and Entei appeared on the beach.

"Which one of you trainers wants to battle me next?" Molly asked.

"I guess Brock couldn't beat her," Ash shot back.

Molly shrugged. "Which one of you is a stronger trainer than your friend?"

Misty grabbed Ash's sleeve. "Leave this to me, Ash."

Molly raised an eyebrow. "Who are you?"

"I'm Misty. I'm a Water Pokémon trainer," she said. "I used to be a gym leader in Cerulean City."

"You mean you don't have to be a grown up to be a gym leader?" Molly replied.

"You can become anything you wish Molly," Entei said.

Ash watched, astonished, as Molly transformed into a girl about the same age as Misty. She wore a white dress with a blue bow around her neck.

"Much better," Molly said. "Now let's battle!"

Misty leaned toward Ash. "The real Molly must still be up in that mansion with your mother. Hurry up and find them Ash! I'll stay here."

Ash nodded. There was another crystal staircase in the distance. It was worth a try. As he and Pikachu ran away, he hoped that Misty could distract Molly long enough.

"Pikachu and I are coming, Mom," Ash said under his breath. "It won't be long now!"

Chapter Twelve

Misty's Underwater Battle

Misty didn't know what to expect from this battle. Molly looked pretty harmless in her new form. Still, Molly had to be pretty powerful to beat Brock. And having Entei there wasn't going to help Misty's concentration at all.

I'll do what I do best, Misty thought. She took a deep breath. "Since I'm a Water Pokémon Trainer, I'm going to use Water Pokémon for this battle," Misty announced.

Molly smiled. "Okay. I'll only use Water Pokémon, too."

Suddenly, the water in the ocean began

to rise. Misty clutched Togepi tightly. Before she knew it, the water seemed to be all around them. Misty couldn't even see the sky above.

We're going to drown, was her first panicked thought. But then she realized, incredibly, that she could breathe. She looked down at Togepi.

"Togi," gurgled the Pokémon. Togepi was fine, too.

"I get it," Misty said. Her voice sounded normal under the water. "You can make anything happen here, can't you?"

Molly wasn't interested in talking. "I'll pick first," she cried. "Help me out, Kingdra."

Molly held out a Poké Ball, and Kingdra swam out. The blue-green Pokémon looked like a sea horse. Misty thought it might be the evolved form of Seadra. It looked a lot like Seadra, only tougher.

Misty threw out one of her own Poké Balls. "Go, Goldeen!"

A beautiful orange-and-white Pokémon appeared. Goldeen had a frilly tail, fins on either side of its body, and a single horn in the front of its head. Goldeen was graceful, but Misty knew its attacks were tough.

Kingdra attacked first. Dark clouds of smoke poured from its snout and rippled through the blue water. The Smoke Screen Attack surrounded Goldeen. Misty's Pokémon couldn't make a move in the darkness.

"Move right into a Head Butt, Kingdra!" Molly called out.

Kingdra swam through the smoke screen and collided into Goldeen with the top of its head. The blow sent Goldeen somersaulting backward through the water.

"Goldeen, Fury Attack!" Misty countered.

Goldeen focused on Kingdra and began to zoom through the water. Misty held her breath. If it made contact with Kingdra, this round would be over.

But Kingdra zipped out of Goldeen's path. It happened so fast Misty almost didn't see it.

Goldeen paused, confused. Kingdra moved back in and slammed into Goldeen with its snout.

That powerful blow was all it took. Goldeen flopped over in a faint.

"Good job, Goldeen," Misty said. She called Goldeen safely back to its Poké Ball.

No wonder Brock couldn't beat her, Misty said. *Her Pokémon are super powerful. And she knows how to give commands.*

Misty took out another Poké Ball. "Go, Staryu!" she cried.

The star-shaped Pokémon burst from the ball just as Molly's next Pokémon appeared in the water. "I need you, Mantine," Molly said.

Mantine had a flat, sleek body that was blue on top and white on its underside. A ribbonlike tail floated in the water behind it. The two flat fins on its sides looked almost like airplane wings.

"Mantine, Tackle Staryu," Molly called out.

Mantine charged through the water, but Staryu was ready for it. Staryu swam away as fast as it could.

Mantine gave chase, but it couldn't catch up. Molly changed her strategy.

"Mantine, use Whirlpool!" she yelled.

Mantine began to swim in circles around Staryu. Molly's Pokémon swam faster and faster until a swirling funnel of water surrounded Staryu.

"It's trapped!" Misty exclaimed.

"Now use Bubble Beam," Molly told Mantine.

Mantine shot a stream of bubbles from its mouth. The bubbles pushed their way through the whirlpool.

If those bubbles hit Staryu, this is over, Misty thought.

But Staryu wasn't out yet. It swam through the whirlpool with all its might, escaping the trap. Staryu charged at Mantine.

Wham! The two Pokémon slammed into each other.

Misty let out a sigh of relief. Staryu hadn't fainted.

I'm not done with Molly yet, Misty thought, *but I hope Ash finds his mom soon. . . .*

As Misty battled Molly, Ash and Pikachu climbed up another crystal staircase. This one led to another door.

Ash took a deep breath. *No more dream-worlds. Please let this be Mom.*

Ash opened the door. He and Pikachu stepped inside what looked like a little girl's room. A little girl was sleeping on a crystal bed. And there, next to her, was his mom!

"Mom!" Ash cried. He and Pikachu ran to the bed. "Are you okay?"

But Delia just stared at Ash with a confused look in her eyes.

Ash gently shook his mom's shoulders. "Mom, Mom, it's me. Snap out of it!"

"Pika!" added Pikachu.

Delia looked from Ash to Pikachu. Suddenly, her eyes brightened.

"Ash! Pikachu! It's you!" She hugged them both to her. "But what were you thinking, coming to this place? I wish I knew where you got such a reckless streak."

Ash smiled. This was definitely his mom, all right. "I guess I got it from you."

Ash looked down at the little girl. "Is that Molly?" he asked.

Delia nodded.

"Have you seen any Unown around?" Ash asked.

"Do you mean the Pokémon that brought me here?" Delia asked. "No, it left a while ago."

"That Pokémon was Entei," said Ash. "The Unown are the Pokémon that made Entei and turned this place crystal from things in Molly's imagination."

Delia gazed at the sleeping girl. She looked so peaceful. "That's hard to believe."

Pikachu tugged at Ash's sleeve. *"Pika! Pika!"*

"Pikachu's right," Ash said. "We've got to get you and Molly out of here."

Molly stirred at the sound of her name. She opened her eyes and sat up.

"I was dreaming, Mama. Who are you?" she asked Ash.

Delia looked into Molly's eyes. "Please listen to me carefully, Molly. We can't stay here in this tower. It's not safe."

Molly folded her arms. "I like it here. It's pretty. I don't need to go outside. I have you and Entei to take care of me."

"I'm very sorry Molly, but I'm not your real mama," Delia said gently. "You'll have to know the truth sooner or later. I'm really Ash's mother."

"No!" Molly screamed.

As Molly's cries filled the air, crystals began to swirl around the room. Giant points of crystal began to spring up from the floor. The room shook like it was being struck by an earthquake.

"I won't let you leave!" Molly yelled.

Chapter Thirteen

Ash vs. Entei

The whole mansion trembled, and Ash felt himself being hurled across the room. Sharp crystal points rose up around him like bars in a jail cell.

Ash scanned the scene. Pikachu had been tossed aside with him. But his mom was separated from him by sharp crystal bars.

"Mom!" Ash yelled. "I'm coming!"

Ash and Pikachu slipped between the crystal points and ran toward his mother. He grabbed his mom's hand, and the three of them broke into a run. Ash saw another staircase up ahead.

"Over there!" Ash pulled his mom

toward the stairs. Sharp crystal spears shot up with each step they took.

"We can't leave without Molly," said Delia. "She doesn't realize what she's doing. She's just a little girl."

Suddenly, Entei and Molly blocked their path. It was like they came out of nowhere.

Molly pointed at Ash. "That boy is taking Mama away," she told Entei.

Entei stared at Ash. "Leave her here and leave this place."

Ash stared right back. "I can't do that. She's my mom!"

"No, in this place she's Molly's mother," Entei replied.

"I don't care what you say!" Ash said firmly.

Entei wouldn't be swayed. "She is staying here. Leave this place immediately or you will be made to leave."

Ash knew there was only one way to solve this. Entei might be something out of Molly's dreams, but it was still a Pokémon. Ash grabbed a Poké Ball from his pocket.

"Totodile, I choose you!" Ash cried.

The small Water Pokémon appeared in a blaze of light.

"Do you think you can beat me?" Entei asked.

"I won't lose to some little girl's imaginary friend. You're just an illusion," Ash said.

"See if this is an illusion!" Entei said, raising a shaggy eyebrow. "Fool!"

"Totodile, Water Gun!" Ash cried.

Totodile obeyed, and Entei dove out of the way of the water stream. Then it opened its mouth and unleashed a blast of purple flames.

"Totodile!" the Water Pokémon cried out as it was scorched by the flames.

Ash quickly called back Totodile. "If water won't work, I'll fight fire with fire. Cyndaquil, you're up!"

The little Fire Pokémon flew out of its Poké Ball and launched right into a Flame-thrower Attack. Red-hot flames poured out of Cyndaquil's mouth.

The flames hit Entei, but the larger Pokémon did not flinch. It countered with another strange purple Fire Attack.

Cyndaquil cringed as the fiery attack hit its mark. Ash quickly called Cyndaquil back into its Poké Ball.

"Do you think I am just an illusion now?" Entei asked.

Ash didn't back down. "You haven't proven anything. Molly dreamed you up. You're not real."

"No! You're wrong!" Molly cried.

Once again, the mansion seemed to respond to Molly's anger. Crystal points shot through the air like arrows. The crystal spears that had risen out of the floor began to grow taller and taller.

"I am this girl's father!" Entei roared. "And I must protect my daughter."

Pikachu jumped in front of Entei. Sparks sizzled on its cheeks. The Fire Pokémon leaped at Pikachu.

"Pikaaaaa!" Pikachu aimed a bolt of lightning at Entei.

The shock illuminated Entei's body in midair. But Entei managed to land on all fours. It hurled a purple fireball at Pikachu.

"Pikachu!" Ash warned.

Pikachu jumped out of the way. It zapped Entei with another lightning bolt.

Entei growled in fury and countered with another ball of purple flame. Pikachu dodged out of the way again and bolted across the floor. Crystal spears shot up all around Pikachu as it ran.

Entei hurled one purple fireball after another. Pikachu evaded them all. Finally, it found itself backed up against a window.

Entei paused and readied itself for a final blow. Ash watched as Entei built up energy for another fireball. Pikachu lay slumped against the wall, exhausted.

Ash ran toward Pikachu. He couldn't let Entei attack Pikachu one more time. He knew Pikachu couldn't take it.

"Pikachu!" Ash yelled as he threw his body in front of Pikachu's.

Ash felt flames singe his face as a fireball zoomed past them, blasting a hole through the crystal wall.

"Got you, Pikachu." Ash grabbed the little yellow Pokémon.

But a cold wind sprang up inside the room. Ash's stomach lurched as the wind carried him and Pikachu out of the hole.

"Noooo!" Ash yelled.

Chapter Fourteen

Charizard to the Rescue

Ash held onto Pikachu tightly as they plummeted to the earth below.

Ash closed his eyes.

Suddenly, Ash felt two strong arms grab him. His eyes flew open.

"Charizard!" Ash cried.

A combination Fire and Flying Pokémon, Charizard was one of Ash's strongest Pokémon. Ash hadn't seen Charizard in weeks, since he'd left it to train in the Charicific Valley. Now it held Ash and Pikachu tightly as it flew outside Hale Mansion.

"Charizard, you came for me," Ash said.

Charizard nodded.

"Thank you," Ash said.

"Pikachu!" Pikachu said happily.

Ash pointed to the crystal palace. "We've got to get back in there. My mom needs help, Brock and Misty are in there, and there's a little girl who needs us."

Charizard nodded again and flew back through the hole in the wall.

"Ash! You're okay," his mom cried.

"Yeah," Molly said. She looked relieved.

Entei eyed Charizard. "What is this thing?"

Ash and Pikachu climbed down from Charizard's back. "Charizard is my friend," Ash said.

"Friend?" Entei asked.

"All of my Pokémon are my friends," Ash said. "We work together like a family."

Entei wasn't impressed. "Then I will defeat your family, too," said the shaggy beast.

Charizard's eyes narrowed at Entei's words. That sounded like a challenge.

Charizard flew toward Entei, ready to attack. Entei charged ahead. The two Pokémon crashed together. Charizard was strong, but Entei was stronger. Charizard went skidding backward across the crystal floor.

Bam! Charizard knocked into Ash and

Pikachu. The force sent him and Pikachu blasting through the hole in the wall.

Pikachu grabbed onto Ash's back. Ash reached out just in time and grabbed onto the wall. His legs dangled over the side of the crystal mansion.

Ash felt his fingers slipping on the slick crystal. He couldn't hold on much longer. He could see Charizard inside, but the Pokémon was knocked out cold.

"Gotcha, Ash!" said a familiar voice.

Ash looked up. Misty grabbed onto his hands. Brock was behind her, pulling them up.

"You guys made it!" Ash cried.

"We're like family, too," Misty said.

Misty and Brock strained to pull up Ash and Pikachu. Suddenly, another cold wind blew through the hole.

"Oh, no!" yelled Misty and Brock as they lurched forward on the slippery crystal floor.

Then Ash heard another familiar voice.

"I'd tell you to prepare for trouble, but it looks like you're already in trouble," said Jessie.

"Team Rocket!" Ash cried.

Chapter Fifteen

Charizard vs. Entei

Jessie, James, and Meowth gave one heave. Together, they pulled Brock, Misty, Ash, and Pikachu safely back inside the mansion.

"Team Rocket is helping out again!" cheered Jessie, James, and Meowth together.

Ash couldn't believe it. Team Rocket was usually getting him into trouble, not out of it. "Why did you save us?" Ash asked them. "You're bad guys."

Jessie shrugged. "Well . . ."

". . . ya see . . ." said Meowth.

". . . it's really very simple," finished James.

73

"If anything happened to you," said Meowth, "we'd have to get a real job."

"Uh, thanks, I guess," Ash said. He scanned the room. Charizard was back on its feet. Molly stood next to his mother, holding her hand. He approached the little girl. "Please come with us, Molly. We'll all be your friends."

Molly frowned. Three crystal Pokémon appeared next to her. A transparent Flaaffy, Teddiursa, and Phanpy stood by her side.

"I already have all the friends I need," she said. "I don't need you. Go away!"

Entei reacted to Molly's cry by hurling a purple fireball at Ash.

"Charizard!" Ash yelled. He jumped out of the way and scrambled on top of Charizard's back.

Charizard aimed a burst of fire at Entei. The shaggy Pokémon leaped up, avoiding the flame.

Charizard and Entei faced each other. Delia stepped up to Entei.

"I don't care if you're a real Pokémon or not," Delia told the Pokémon. "You can't take the place of her real father!"

"Molly wants me to stay with her," Entei replied. "I must do what she wishes."

Then Entei opened its mouth, and a huge purple ball of flame began to form. Charizard's mouth opened, and an orange fireball formed there.

The two fireballs met in midair and exploded with a huge bang. Splintered pieces of crystal showered everyone in the room.

"Let's take this outside!" Ash shouted. He didn't want anyone to get hurt — not even Team Rocket. Besides, Charizard would have an advantage outside. Entei was strong, but it couldn't fly.

Charizard steered through the hole in the wall. The Flying Pokémon darted between the blue crystal towers. Below, Ash saw the pink crystal pieces that looked like flower petals. They had looked beautiful from a distance, but up close they were sharp and dangerous.

Entei charged out of the hole after Charizard, landing on top of the first blue tower. Charizard circled Entei, then unleashed a fiery flame at the shaggy Pokémon.

Entei had no choice. It leaped from the tower.

"Papa!" Molly cried.

Immediately, a horizontal shard of crystal sprung out from the side of the tower. Entei landed squarely on the piece of crystal.

Molly won't let Entei fall, Ash realized.

Entei seemed to realize the same thing. It jumped toward Charizard. Another crystal platform extended out, and Entei landed safely again. Now it opened its mouth and sent a purple fireball hurling at Charizard.

Ash clutched Charizard's back as his Pokémon swooped down and escaped the attack. In the meantime, Entei jumped through the air, getting closer and closer. Crystal appeared under Entei's feet with each leap.

Charizard turned in midair and dove down at Entei, then let loose with another Flamethrower Attack. Entei jumped out of the way, but not before sending a purple fireball hurtling toward Charizard.

Ash held tightly onto Charizard's back as his Pokémon veered out of the way. Charizard was flying fast, but Entei was right behind it. Molly's Pokémon seemed to fly itself as it jumped from crystal to crystal.

Again and again, the Pokémon traded brutal attacks. Ash wondered how long the fierce battle would last. Charizard and Entei couldn't seem to hit each other. They were both too fast, too agile.

Entei landed on top of one of the blue crystal towers. The Pokémon paused to consider its next move. Charizard took advantage of the brief pause. It flew past Entei, blasting it with a powerful Flamethrower Attack.

Entei roared as the burning flames made contact. Charizard swooped down and landed on the opposite tower. Ash knew it would need to rest a second before it continued the fight.

But maybe the fight wouldn't have to continue. "Please, Entei. Listen to me," Ash called out.

Entei didn't reply.

"If you really care about Molly, you would let us take her out of here," Ash said. "She needs to be in the real world, where people can take care of her. If we don't do something now, she'll be alone forever!"

"It may not be right," Entei said, "but it is what Molly wishes. And I will do what Molly wishes me to do."

Then Entei opened its mouth, and a huge purple ball of flame began to form. This one was three times as big as anything Entei had ever delivered before.

"Let's get out of here, Charizard!" Ash yelled, but it was too late. Ash buried his head in Charizard's back as the fiery purple energy slammed into Charizard's body. There was a loud explosion, and the air filled with black smoke.

Ash coughed as the smoke filled his lungs, but soon felt the cold wind on his face again. He opened his eyes.

They had made it! Charizard was flying back into the mansion through the hole in the wall.

Entei bounded in right behind him. Before Charizard could react, Molly's Pokémon sent another ball of purple flame spiraling toward them.

Charizard bucked up, tossing Ash off its back. But the lizard Pokémon couldn't get away in time. As Ash scrambled to his feet, he saw that Charizard had been knocked out. The big Pokémon lay on its side with its eyes closed.

Entei jumped over to Charizard and placed a paw on the Pokémon's neck.

"Now to finish it," Entei said somberly.

"Charizard! No!" Ash cried. Entei was too powerful. He couldn't lose Charizard like this. Not after it had risked everything to save him.

Molly let go of Delia's hand. She looked at Ash's stricken face. She looked at Charizard, who lay helpless on the floor.

Then Molly took a step forward.

"Stop!" Molly yelled. "No more fighting Entei — I mean Papa. No more."

Chapter Sixteen

Battle Against the Unown

Entei backed away from Charizard. "Whatever you wish, Molly," said the Pokémon.

Relief flooded over Ash. He ran to Molly. "Thank you so much. You did the right thing."

"You're a great Pokémon trainer, Molly," Brock said.

"Really?" asked Molly.

Brock nodded. "You beat me. Your Phanpy's Rollout Attack was seriously strong."

"Mantine's Whirlpool was awesome,"

added Misty. "I bet you could become a gym leader easy if you wanted to."

Team Rocket nodded from the sidelines.

"See, Molly?" said Ash. "We always battle hard, but we always stay friends — 'cause we all love Pokémon."

Molly seemed to consider this.

"Come with us, Molly," Ash said.

"Outside, the battles may be hard," Misty added.

"But the friends are real," Brock finished.

Ash's mom grabbed Molly's hand. "Let's go, Molly," she said.

Molly nodded. "Okay. I'll go with you."

Molly's three crystal Pokémon, Flaaffy, Teddiursa, and Phanpy, vanished into thin air. The crystal walls around them seemed to melt away, like ice turning into water.

"Cool!" Ash said. "Maybe the Unown are going away."

"I was born to be the father who would make you happy here." Entei said. "If you would be happier outside in the real world, I must go."

But things suddenly got much worse.

The melting walls turned to solid crystal again. More sharp spears rose up from the floor.

Ash took out his Poké Gear. "Professor Oak! Something's happening!"

Oak's face appeared on the screen.

"The Unown have generated so much chaotic energy that they can no longer control it," said the professor. "The crystal is coming toward the Pokémon Center now. Listen to me, get out of there or you could be trapped forever!"

"We'll try," Ash replied. He picked up Molly and put her on Charizard's back. "Charizard, take care of Molly. Don't let go of her. We've got to find a way out of here."

Pikachu ran ahead, dodging through crystal spears. Ash saw where it was leading them. A hole in the floor led to a staircase.

"Let's go!" Ash yelled, but a ring of crystal spears popped up around the opening, blocking their way. Entei stepped up and hurled a purple flame at the crystals. It was enough to knock them down for a minute — all the time they needed.

"This way!" shouted Ash, and the others

followed as he and Pikachu rushed down the steps.

"Maybe we can get out through the greenhouse," Ash called back to his friends. "We can get Molly and Mom to safety and then figure out a way to stop these things."

It wasn't much of a plan, Ash knew. But he realized he didn't even know what the Unown looked like. How was he supposed to stop them?

Soon they reached the bottom of the stairs. Ash started to run for the greenhouse door.

Then he stopped.

High-pitched chirps assaulted his ears. The sounds came from tiny Pokémon that swirled around the middle of the room. There must have been hundreds of them, Ash guessed. Each Pokémon looked kind of like an alphabet letter, but each seemed strangely alive.

"The Unown," Ash said, amazed.

The swirling mass of Unown blocked their way out of the mansion.

Ash charged ahead.

An invisible barrier pushed him backward. The Unown began to swirl even faster and chatter even louder, as though they sensed Ash's assault.

"Some kind of barrier is protecting them," Brock mused out loud.

"Try to break through it," Ash said. "Go, Charizard!"

Charizard handed Molly to Ash's mom. Then Charizard flew full force into the mass of Unown.

Slam! The invisible barrier sent Charizard careening backward.

That only made Charizard angrier. The Lizard Pokémon assaulted the Unown with a stream of fire.

At first, the fire blasted a hole through the wall of Unown. But the hole quickly closed up, and an invisible force sent Charizard reeling backward once again. The Fire Pokémon slammed into the floor with a thud.

Ash turned to Pikachu. "Your turn," Ash said. "Use Thunderbolt!"

Pikachu ran up to the dancing mass of Unown. The air sizzled as Pikachu built up energy for the Electric Attack. Then it unleashed a Thunderbolt and aimed it at the Unown.

Each of the Unown glowed an eerie yellow. But Pikachu's attack did not stop their dance. Charizard jumped back to its feet and ran to Pikachu's side. The Lizard Pokémon aimed another fire blast at the Unown.

Ash watched in amazement. Nothing could withstand a double attack from Pikachu and Charizard — nothing. Nothing, that is, except the Unown.

Pikachu and Charizard both went flying backward. Ash knew what Professor Oak meant when he said that the Unown could not control their power. They were dancing around like kernels in a popcorn machine.

The Unown began to swirl around faster than before. They almost seemed angry. Ash had to jump to the side as a sharp crystal rose out of the floor next to him. More crystals were popping up all over the room. From the corner of his eye, Ash saw his mom pick up Molly and run for cover. Misty and Brock stood by, ready to help. Jessie, James, and Meowth huddled in a corner, staring at the Unown with disbelief in their eyes.

"This is a very dangerous situation," Jessie said.

"Well," Meowth said. "Whenever the going gets tough, Team Rocket gets going."

"I choose leaving!" James shouted above the Unown's screeches.

Ash had to focus. Charizard and Pikachu were down, but not out. They'd be on their feet soon. But Ash wasn't sure they could stop the Unown by themselves. And where was Entei?

The sound of shattering crystal answered Ash's thought. Entei burst through a crystal wall. He looked at the Unown. Then he turned to Molly.

"Molly, I was happy and proud to be your father," Entei said slowly. "The last thing I can do for you is to take you out of this place."

"Entei," Molly said softly. Tears filled her eyes.

Entei turned and faced the Unown. An explosion of purple flame burst from the Pokémon and thudded into the barrier. Ash could see the barrier waver, but Entei's attack still wasn't strong enough to make a dent.

"I was born of your dreams," Entei

growled, trying to keep up the attack. "If you believe in me, there's nothing I can't do."

Suddenly, Ash knew what Entei meant. "Molly! You have to believe in Entei. Believe it can stop the Unown."

Molly took a deep breath. "You can do it, Entei. I believe in you."

Entei hurled a purple fireball at the Unown. The purple flames hit the invisible barrier and dissolved once again.

"You can do it!" Molly yelled again.

By now, Pikachu and Charizard were back in the game. They blasted the Unown with a steady stream of electricity and fire. Entei joined them, this time sending a blue ice beam at the Unown.

The electricity, fire, and ice mingled in the air. Together, they hit the Unown's protective force field. A loud explosion rocked the room.

The blast knocked everyone in the room off their feet. Ash instinctively covered his eyes with his arm as the room filled with a bright white light.

Ash struggled to open his eyes. What he saw made him gasp. Entei appeared in the center of the light, like a vision in the air. The Unown glowed brightly around him.

"I've got to go now, Molly," Entei said. "I will miss you. Just keep me close in your dreams."

Molly nodded, too tearful to speak.

Entei dissolved into tiny particles of light. Some of the Unown began to fall to the floor like rain. As each one hit the floor, it turned into a wooden tile. The tiles clattered as they made contact and then lay still.

The tiles dissolved, just as Entei had. The remaining Unown above them began to swirl once again. This time, they formed a funnel of light. Then the funnel swirled up to the ceiling and disappeared.

Chapter Seventeen

Together Again

Hale Mansion was eerily quiet.

"Are they gone?" Ash whispered.

The crystal answered his question. It quickly began to shrink back. In just a few seconds, the room they were in looked like a normal room again. There was no sign of crystal anywhere.

Ash and Pikachu ran to the window. The crystal was vanishing from the fields surrounding the mansion. Instead of shiny glass, Ash saw green grass and colorful flowers everywhere.

"Pika!" exclaimed Pikachu.

Delia carried Molly to the window. Brock, Misty, and Team Rocket joined them.

"Wow," said Misty. "I told you Greenfield is beautiful."

"And it's real," added Brock.

Ash saw that a caravan of police cars was working its way up the road to the mansion.

Jessie nudged Meowth and James. "Well, we can't get out of this tower now," she said.

"Not with all those police around," James agreed.

Meowth sighed. "Guess we're stuck here all alone."

"We should be happy," James said.

"How could we be happy," Meowth said. "We didn't capture one new Pokémon!"

Jessie turned and looked at Molly, who seemed happy for the first time that day.

"I'm happy for that little girl. She was adorable yet indomitable just like me!"

"And that Entei was powerful and in-scrutable, just like me!" said James.

"And that Meowth was lovable just like me!" added Meowth.

"What does it matter if we failed at catching a Pokémon this time?" Jessie asked.

"We'll get another chance to fail next time!" finished James.

Jessie grabbed Meowth and James by the arm. "And so until next time, Team Rocket's fading out again!"

Team Rocket slipped out of the room. Ash didn't even notice. Outside, Professor Oak and Lisa stepped out of a police car. Schuyler came out behind them.

"Molly! Are you all right?" Schuyler called up.

"Molly's fine. We're coming down," Ash called back.

Molly was excited to see Schuyler again. She ran out the door and into Schuyler's arms. Professor Oak looked relieved to see they were all right.

"I see Charizard came to help you," Oak remarked.

Ash beamed at Charizard. "It was kind of a surprise."

Professor Oak smiled. "That's not the only surprise."

Another police car pulled up. A man with long hair and tired eyes stepped out.

"Papa!" Molly cried. She jumped out of Schuyler's arms and ran toward her father.

"Professor Hale?" Ash couldn't believe it.

"The Unown returned him to the research site," Schuyler explained. "Officer Jenny made sure he was brought here as quickly as possible."

Ash smiled as Molly and her dad hugged. It was nice to see the father and daughter reunited.

He walked over to his own mom.

"I'm glad you're okay," he told her.

Ash's mom smiled. "It was quite an adventure."

Ash thought about the events of the last twenty-four hours. He had almost lost his mom. He had seen Pokémon that few people had ever seen before. And he couldn't have made it through without his friends. Brock. Misty. Pikachu. Charizard. Even Team Rocket!

Ash smiled. "It was an amazing adventure, Mom," he said. "I've done some incredible things in the Johto region. But this beats them all!"